Darlison, Aleesah, author.
Krystal's choice

2017
33305238964419
gi   06/02/17

D1092465

UNICORN RIDERS

Krystal's Choice

Aleesah Darlison

Illustrations by
Jill Brailsford

PICTURE WINDOW BOOKS
a capstone imprint

Willow & Obecky

Willow's symbol
- a violet—represents being watchful and faithful

Uniform color
- green

Unicorn
- Obecky has a black opal horn.
- She has the gifts of healing and strength.

Ellabeth & Fayza

Ellabeth's symbol
- a hummingbird—represents energy, persistence, and loyalty

Uniform color
- red

Unicorn
- Fayza has an orange topaz horn.
- She has the gift of speed and can also light the dark with her golden magic.

UNICORN RIDERS

We Ride As One

To my children and all those who believe in unicorns — AD
To my children, Clare and Max — JB

Picture Window Books are published by Capstone,
1710 Roe Crest Drive, North Mankato, Minnesota 56003
www.mycapstone.com

Text © 2017 Aleesah Darlison
Illustrations © 2017 Jill Brailsford

All rights reserved. No part of this publication may be reproduced in whole
or in part, or stored in a retrieval system, or transmitted in any form or by any
means, electronic, mechanical, photocopying, recording, or otherwise, without
written permission of the publisher.

Library of Congress Cataloging-in-Publication Data
Names: Darlison, Aleesah, author. | Brailsford, Jill, illustrator.
Title: Krystal's choice / by Aleesah Darlison; [Jill Brailsford, illustrator].
Description: North Mankato, Minnesota : Picture Window Books, an imprint of
    Capstone Press, [2017] | Series: Unicorn Riders | Summary: Coming from a
    wealthy family, Krystal is finding it hard to adjust to the responsibility
    of being a Unicorn Rider, so when they arrive in the town of Miramar to
    investigate the disappearance of seven children, she changes out of her
    uniform and slips away to explore—and stumbles into a plot to capture the
    unicorns and their riders.
Identifiers: LCCN 2016007997| ISBN 9781479565467 (library binding) |
ISBN 9781479565542 (paperback) | ISBN 9781479584857 (ebook (pdf))
Subjects: LCSH: Unicorns—Juvenile fiction. | Magic—Juvenile fiction. |
    Kidnapping—Juvenile fiction. | Responsibility—Juvenile fiction. |
    Adventure stories. | CYAC: Unicorns—Fiction. | Magic—Fiction. |
    Kidnapping—Fiction. | Responsibility—Fiction. | Adventure and
    adventurers—Fiction. | GSAFD: Adventure stories.
Classification: LCC PZ7.1.D333 Kr 2017 | DDC 813.6—dc23
LC record available at http://lccn.loc.gov/2016007997

Editor: Nikki Potts
Designer: Bobbie Nuytten
Art Director: Nathan Gassman
Production Specialist: Katy LaVigne
The illustrations in this book were created by Jill Brailsford.

Cover design by Walker Books Australia Pty Ltd
Cover images: Rider, symbol and unicorns © Gillian Brailsford 2011;
lined paper © iStockphoto.com/Imageegaml;
parchment © iStockphoto.com/Peter Zelei

The illustrations for this book were created with black pen,
pencil, and digital media.

Design Element: Shutterstock: Slanapotam

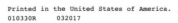

Printed in the United States of America.
010330R   032017

Quinn & Ula

Quinn's symbol
- a butterfly—represents change and lightness

Uniform color
- blue

Unicorn
- Ula has a ruby horn.
- She has the gift of speaking with Quinn using mind-messages.
- She can also sense danger.

Krystal & Estrella

Krystal's symbol
- a diamond—represents perfection, wisdom, and beauty

Uniform color
- purple

Unicorn
- Estrella has a pearl horn.
- She has the gift of enchantment.

The Unicorn Riders' World

The Unicorn Riders of Avamay

Under the guidance of their leader, Jala, the Unicorn Riders and their magical unicorns protect the Kingdom of Avamay from the threats of evil Lord Valerian.

Decades ago, Lord Valerian forcefully took over the neighboring kingdom of Obeera. He began capturing every magical creature across the eight kingdoms. Luckily, King Perry saved four of Avamay's unicorns. He asked the unicorns to help protect Avamay. And that's when ordinary girls were chosen to be the first Unicorn Riders.

A Rider is chosen when her name and likeness appear in The Choosing Book, which is guarded by Jala. It holds the details of all the past, present, and future Riders. No one can see who the future Riders will be until it is time for a new Rider to be chosen. Only then will The Choosing Book display her details.

• CHAPTER 1 •

WITH HER LONG HAIR streaming behind her, Krystal rode Estrella into the village square. "Behold Estrella, Avamay's most dazzling unicorn!" she cried. "Watch her perform her tricks. Admire her stunning beauty!"

The crowd parted, forming a circle around Krystal and Estrella. Krystal had spent hours combing her unicorn's coat and braiding her golden mane and tail with ribbons. She hoped the people of Stillmet would be impressed.

Stillmet sat at the base of the Effervescent Falls. It was a poor village. Recently a terrible flood had washed through it, damaging many of the houses in its path. Queen Heart had sent the Riders to help.

Estrella whinnied, rising onto her hind legs while Krystal clung to her back. With every nudge of Krystal's knees the unicorn obeyed — stepping, rearing, and turning like a dancer.

The crowd gasped in wonder. Krystal smiled. She had wanted to make them happy. They'd had such a terrible time lately.

"E, use your magic," Krystal whispered.

Every unicorn had a special skill. Estrella's was the ability to enchant others. Now, as Krystal held one hand high, Estrella pirouetted on her hind legs and sent a shower of magical sparks from her pearl horn over the crowd.

"Amazing!" they exclaimed. "Breathtaking!"

Estrella landed on all fours. Her pearly-white sparks dissolved, breaking the spell. The crowd clapped and cheered. Krystal slid off Estrella and greeted the villagers, shaking hands with many of them.

How wonderful it is to make others happy, Krystal thought. *To entertain them and help them forget their troubles.*

Not that she got much chance to entertain people with Estrella's dancing tricks. Jala, the Unicorn Riders' Leader, didn't approve of performances like the one Krystal had just given. She would have called it showing off.

The crowd slowly left. Ellabeth trudged over carrying a bucket of sudsy water. Her red Unicorn Rider's uniform was smudged with dirt, as was her forehead. "That was a nice thing to do. Are you ready to help now? There's a cottage over here that needs cleaning," Ellabeth said.

"Well, it's not as glamorous as dancing with a unicorn," Krystal replied with a grin, "but I guess I can help."

Ellabeth laughed. "You're too kind," she said. "Come on, then."

The two girls fell into step together. "You know, you'd better not let Jala catch you wasting Estrella's magic like that," Ellabeth said. "You'll get in trouble."

"I was only trying to cheer up the villagers," Krystal said.

"Yeah, but you know what Jala's like with rules," replied Ellabeth. "This is the place. In you go."

Krystal eyed the cottage Ellabeth pointed to. She wrinkled her nose. "It smells awful," she said.

Ellabeth shrugged. "The others aren't complaining," she answered.

Krystal glanced at Quinn and Willow, the other Unicorn Riders. Both wore their uniforms. Quinn's was pale blue with the symbol of a butterfly embroidered on the front. Willow's was green with

the symbol of a purple violet. While Quinn swept the stone steps of a house nearby, Willow, the Head Rider, helped the woman who lived there replant her vegetable garden.

Krystal eyed the cottage once more. She still wasn't sure she was up to the task. "I need a drink first," she said. "I'll be back in a minute. Promise." She ran off, leaving Ellabeth shaking her head.

Krystal crouched by the river, cupping the cool water in her hands to drink. "I'm a Unicorn Rider," she murmured. "I protect the kingdom from evil threats like Lord Valerian. Cleaning cottages isn't what being a Unicorn Rider is about. This is all too hard."

Krystal began to turn when she heard footsteps crunching on the rocks behind her. Willow, Ellabeth, and Quinn approached her and sat beside her.

"Are you finding the work difficult?" Willow asked.

Krystal nodded. "Why can't we use unicorn magic to fix everything?" she asked.

Willow laughed. "Because magic can't solve every problem," she said. "Sometimes hard work is the only answer."

"I'm no good at hard work," Krystal said.

Quinn hugged Krystal. "Sure you are," she said. "You always work hard to train Estrella and groom her."

"I guess," said Krystal. She studied the calluses on her hands. Once, her hands had been soft and her nails painted. Not any more.

Before she had been chosen to be a Rider, Krystal's playground had been her parents' huge country estate. She'd had servants, nannies, and a tutor. There had been beautiful dresses, endless parties, and ponies to ride. Her wealthy parents had showered their only child with love and gifts, making her life a perfect fairytale.

Everything had changed when Krystal's name appeared in The Choosing Book. The Choosing Book held the details of all past, present, and future Riders, only the future Riders' names couldn't be seen until it was time for a new Rider to be chosen. Only then would The Choosing Book display the details.

Of course, Krystal had been delighted when her name appeared in the great book. Every girl in the kingdom dreamed of becoming a Unicorn Rider. Only a handful were ever chosen.

But being a Rider was different from how Krystal had imagined it. She had to challenge herself and face great dangers. She had to share everything with the other Riders, including a bedroom with Ellabeth. She even had to do daily chores.

I miss my old life, Krystal thought. *I miss my family. I'm no good at cleaning. It's just not my thing. Does that make me a bad Rider?*

"Ah, the adventurous life of a Unicorn Rider," Willow said. "It has its ups and downs."

"I love the adventure," Krystal said. "It's the dullness I can't stand."

"We can't all shine all the time," Ellabeth said.

Krystal was about to tell Ellabeth to stop teasing her when the sound of an approaching horse made her look up.

"The Queen's messenger," said Krystal. She recognized the purple coat, the gold sash.

"Honorable Riders," announced the messenger, bowing in his saddle. "The Queen approaches."

• CHAPTER 2 •

"LET'S GREET THE QUEEN in the village square," Willow said.

Krystal dusted off her faded purple uniform. The ragged diamond symbol made her frown. Her diamond was meant to stand for clarity and perfection.

It certainly doesn't look like that now, she thought. *I can't let Queen Heart see me like this.* She backed away. "Give me a minute, okay?" she said.

"Again?" Ellabeth said, her hands on her hips.

"Yes, again," Krystal said before rushing off.

Krystal sprinted to the hut where the Riders were staying. Once there, she scrubbed her face and brushed her hair until they were clean and bright.

She straightened her uniform as best she could, though it didn't help much.

Outside Krystal found Estrella grazing with the other unicorns: Obecky, Fayza, and Ula. She straightened Estrella's ribbons and braids. "Now, E, use your magic to make us both look amazing," she said.

Estrella sent a shower of magical sparks from her pearl horn over the both of them.

Krystal smiled. "I feel better already," she said. "And I'm sure I look better, too." She leaped onto Estrella. Another idea struck her. "E, how about you give the other unicorns some magic, too."

Estrella obeyed. Soon, all of the unicorns looked stunning. Their coats gleamed. Their manes and tails shimmered more brightly than ever.

"Come on, all of you. Let's show them how beautiful unicorns can really look," Krystal said. She cantered up to the village square on Estrella. Obecky, Fayza, and Ula followed close behind.

As she arrived at the square, Krystal was shocked to see Queen Heart dressed in plain black pants and a navy shirt. She had only ever seen the Queen dressed in the finest silks and always in a skirt or dress. Never in pants.

The villagers were all focused on the Queen and didn't notice Krystal and the unicorns.

"I am thrilled with the Unicorn Riders' efforts and with you, my wonderful people, in rebuilding Stillmet," the Queen said. "You have shown patience, commitment, and humbleness working together. What would we do without the Riders and their unicorns? They inspire us. They show us what dedication means."

Krystal moved closer to the gathering crowd. Her heart filled with pride at the Queen's words. It felt heavenly to be appreciated. It made everything worthwhile.

"No one is above helping out," Queen Heart continued. "That's why I am here today working alongside my people."

The crowd murmured and pointed at Krystal and the unicorns with Estrella's magic whirling around them and shimmering in the sunlight.

Willow's eyes went wide. "Get down!" she mouthed to Krystal.

Krystal frowned. *Why is she angry? I'm only trying to look nice.*

Queen Heart turned around. "Oh, Krystal, it's so good of you to join us. My, don't you and the unicorns look dazzling today."

A hand squeezed Krystal's knee. "A word?" Willow hissed up at her. "And cut the magic."

Krystal slid down off Estrella. Willow instructed Quinn and Ellabeth to lead the unicorns back to their stables then motioned for Krystal to follow her.

"What are you doing?" Willow demanded when they were alone. "You just upstaged the Queen."

Krystal winced. "Was it really that bad? Queen Heart didn't seem to mind."

"Queen Heart was being kind. Do you know what that word means?"

How can she ask such a thing? She makes me feel like a naughty child, thought Krystal. "Of course I do," she replied, crossing her arms.

"Not to mention that you were misusing Estrella's magic," Willow added. "Jala wouldn't approve."

"I was trying to make a good impression," Krystal insisted. "To make us look good for Queen Heart." It was important that Willow believed her.

At that moment, the Queen, followed by Quinn and Ellabeth, approached. "Riders, I must speak with you right away," she said. "Although I am here to assist the villagers, there is another reason for my visit."

Krystal's eyes lit up. She was happy for the change of subject and for the possibility of an adventure. The Riders spent much of their time traveling throughout the kingdom at the service of the Queen, solving problems and protecting the people of Avamay. Especially from Lord Valerian. "Is it a mission?" Krystal asked.

Queen Heart nodded. "An envoy has returned from Miramar with disturbing reports of children disappearing," she said. "I want you to travel there to find out more. Lord Valerian has been quiet lately. We must remember, he may have a hand in this. You know he likes stirring up trouble."

"How many children are missing, so far?" Ellabeth asked.

"At least seven," Queen Heart said. "Perhaps more. We're still trying to piece information together. I sent the city leaders a message via Belmont, our messenger falcon, to say you would be in Miramar as soon as possible."

"Miramar!" Krystal gasped.

She had always dreamed of visiting the famous Silver City. Miramar was known for its silver and jewelry making. It was filled with Avamayan culture, precious artworks, and wealth.

"We haven't finished our work here yet," Quinn pointed out.

"My soldiers will look after things until you return," Queen Heart replied.

Willow nodded. "It's getting late, but if we leave now, we'll be in Miramar tonight," she said.

"Yay. A mission!" Ellabeth and Krystal cheered. If there was one thing that could unite the girls, it was the possibility of an adventure.

The Riders set out with a cry, "We ride as one." Willow and confident Obecky led the way. Not long into their journey, black clouds billowed across the sky. Lightning flashed and thunder rumbled. Estrella danced about and whinnied in terror.

"Can't you calm her down?" Ellabeth shouted over the thunder. "She's upsetting the others."

"She can't help it," Krystal said. "You know storms make her nervous."

"Obecky can use her calming magic," Willow said. "I don't want to exhaust her when we still have a long way to travel, but a little magic can't hurt. Obecky, use your magic."

Obecky obeyed, sending a shower of gray-blue sparks over unhappy Estrella. The unicorn gave a long whinny of relief and stopped her prancing.

"She should be fine now," Willow said. "Let's continue on."

The storm continued to rage. At times the thunder boomed so loud the Riders had to cover their ears. The steady rain soaked them to the skin, making them tremble with cold. Even with Obecky's magic, poor Estrella grew increasingly distressed as night set in.

Ellabeth asked, "Can Fayza lead? Her magic will light the night and show us the way."

Fayza's special skill was her speed and her ability to create light with her magical horn.

"Why can't E lead?" Krystal asked. "It might settle her down."

"Fayza is the fastest and can light the way," Ellabeth argued.

"She's also clumsy," Krystal said. "These roads are slippery. We have to be careful."

"I'd rather Fayza led," Willow said. "We'll just take it slowly. Krystal, you ride Estrella at the back so she doesn't upset the others. Come on, let's keep going."

Krystal bit her lip so she wouldn't say anything more. She told herself she was tired, and it didn't matter that Estrella had to ride behind the others.

"Never mind," Krystal said as she comforted her unicorn. "We'll have a turn another time. You take it easy now."

The Unicorn Riders pressed wearily on. Fayza's magic whirled from her topaz horn, lighting the night with a honey-gold glow. The rain poured and the wind howled. Several times they stopped to shelter beneath trees when the storm became too dangerous. It was difficult, but they kept going, crossing swollen rivers, valleys, and plains on their way to Miramar.

● CHAPTER 3 ●

DAWN WAS BREAKING WHEN the riders arrived in the Silver City the next morning. The storm had delayed them many hours. Krystal and the others were cold, wet, and dirty. Estrella's braids had come undone during the ride, and her mane was knotted. Her coat was splattered with mud. Riding at the back of the group had done her no favors.

Krystal was disappointed she wasn't making a grander entrance into the beautiful city. She considered telling Estrella to use her enchantment magic to make them both look better, but she quickly dismissed the idea. She knew it wasn't allowed.

27

"What's up?" Ellabeth asked as they trotted side by side.

"You wouldn't understand," Krystal replied softly.

"Try me," Ellabeth said.

Krystal sighed. "It's just, my mother used to tell me wonderful tales about Miramar," she said. "I always thought I'd come here in my family's carriage dressed in my best. Not looking like I'd just stepped out of a mud bath."

"Never mind," Ellabeth replied. "Mud washes off. At least you still get to see the city."

"I guess you're right," Krystal said.

Willow led them through the busy cobblestone streets of the city to the Firebird Inn where they

had been told they would find good rooms and good food. There was even a stable out back for the unicorns.

"Unicorns!" yelled the stable boy. His eyes went wide as the girls trotted into the inn's courtyard. "They're beauties, too. Just like the legends say." He stared at Estrella. "You're in poor condition, aren't you girl?"

Krystal slid down off her unicorn and led her to the well for a drink. "We were caught in last night's storm," she said. "She usually looks better than this."

"I'd hope so," said the boy. He tugged a twig from Estrella's mane. "Do you want me to wash and brush her? I'll have her looking good in no time."

"If you want," Krystal replied.

Quinn studied Krystal carefully. "Are you okay?" she asked.

"I'm fine," Krystal answered. "Why?"

"You usually don't let anyone else groom Estrella," Quinn said.

Krystal felt a pang of guilt. What Quinn said was true, but right now she didn't care. Estrella had been hard to manage during the storm, and Krystal was exhausted. Someone else could take care of Estrella this time.

"Nothing's wrong," she told Quinn.

"Hey, is that Krystal?" the stable boy whispered. He nodded toward Ellabeth. "I've heard she's the prettiest Rider of all."

Krystal's chin lifted. "I'm Krystal, and this is Estrella, the prettiest unicorn of all," she replied.

The boy studied her for a moment before grinning. "You almost fooled me!" said the boy. "Come on, that is Krystal, isn't it?"

Krystal stomped her foot. "I'm Krystal," she yelled. "Don't you know anything?"

The boy looked at her doubtfully. "Really?" he asked. With a heavy sigh, Krystal tossed her tangled hair and strode out of the stable. She marched into the inn to ask where her room was. Then she stomped upstairs, threw herself on her bed, and stared at the ceiling.

Moments later, a knock sounded at the door.

"Who is it?" she asked, choking back tears.

A servant entered. Her hair was as black and shiny as a crow's wing. Her eyes were emerald green, and her skin the color of chocolate. If Krystal was golden and light in her beauty, this girl was ebony and night in hers. And yet, she was just a servant dressed in a faded, lemon-colored dress.

"Honorable Rider," the girl said. "I was told to bring you fresh clothes and wash your dirty ones."

"Thanks," said Krystal. "My uniform could use a good cleaning." Krystal picked at her frayed diamond symbol.

"There's a hot bath waiting for you," the girl said as she nodded toward the door. "I added rose petals to help soothe you after your journey."

Krystal fidgeted with her hair. *I must look dreadful,* she thought.

"If you need anything, just ring," the girl said as she pointed to a silver bell on the bedside table. "My name is Rhama." She glanced shyly at Krystal. "I'm so glad you're here. My sister is one of the missing children, and I'm worried sick about her. I hope you find her and the others. We're all relying on you."

Krystal scratched her neck where her uniform itched. She eyed the bathroom door. "We'll do all we can, I promise," she said. "But right now I really need a bath."

"Of course," Rhama said as she bowed her head. "When you're ready, you can meet the others in the lounge downstairs." The girl curtsied again then left.

Krystal took off her coat and uniform, leaving them where they fell. Next door she found a fire blazing and the bath set just as Rhama had said. She slid into the water, the scent of roses floating around her. It felt wonderful. She remembered the baths she'd had every night at home, when baths weren't a special treat.

Am I cut out to be a Unicorn Rider? she wondered. *Could The Choosing Book have made a mistake?*

She thought of all the disasters she'd had during the last few days. Getting into trouble at Stillmet, not being able to calm Estrella during the storm, and not being able to lead the group.

Should I step down as a Rider? It would make things easier if I did.

Krystal scrubbed her hands with the scrubbing brush, trying to remove all trace of rough skin. Still it remained. She tossed the brush onto the mat and stepped out of the bath to dry herself with the plump, white towel warming by the fire.

Back in her room, two outfits had been laid out for her on the bed. One was a plain lemon-yellow dress like Rhama's. The other was something entirely different. It was a long, red velvet dress. Its front was crisscrossed with gold ribbons. Its ruffled, cream-colored sleeves were embroidered with red hearts. Underclothes, socks, and a pair of leather boots were also laid out.

Krystal held the yellow dress against herself and looked at her reflection in the mirror.

Is this Rhama's? she wondered.

She glanced at the red dress on the bed. It was so much prettier than the yellow one.

I know which dress I should wear, Krystal thought. *And I know which dress I want to wear.*

After a moment's hesitation, Krystal put on the red dress. Then she braided her hair in a crown braid. She walked downstairs, found the lounge, and peeked inside. The other Riders were huddled around a table talking. They were still dressed in their uniforms, but drying out nicely beside the fire burning in the hearth. Mugs of steaming hot chocolate sat before them.

Surely they won't miss me if I slip out for just a little while, Krystal thought. *Now is the perfect opportunity for me to explore Miramar on my own. They seem fine without me anyway.*

Krystal studied her dress. She studied the other Riders. Then she tiptoed out the door.

• CHAPTER 4 •

KRYSTAL PASSED ROW AFTER row OF brightly-lit shops with items displayed in their windows. Marble carvers, glass blowers, gem cutters, jewelers, miniature painters, and fabric-dyers. And of course, the silver shops with their finely-crafted jewelry, ornaments, and tableware.

She caught her reflection in a shop window and hardly recognized herself. It had been almost two years since she had worn normal clothes.

Krystal knew what she was doing was wrong. Once a girl became a Unicorn Rider, she always had to wear her uniform and be at the service of the Queen and the Avamayan people. Wearing normal clothes again after all this time felt strange. Wrong. But, oh, how she had missed wearing such fine clothes. It felt good being Krystal Pettigrew and not Krystal, the Unicorn Rider.

Soon Krystal came to the Hibiscus Bazaar. Here, hundreds of stalls sold treasures from across the kingdom, including sweets, nuts, fine silks, tea, spices, and fresh fruit and vegetables.

At one stall she saw a silver and glass-bead bracelet displayed on the jeweler's black velvet mats. Each bead was a different color and pattern. A single charm dangled from the bracelet, a miniature silver peacock. Its tail fanned out and was studded with a gemstone on each feather.

I would love to buy it. If only I had the money, Krystal thought.

Krystal glanced over and spotted the Riders talking to a merchant. Ellabeth turned toward her, but Krystal quickly ducked behind some hanging scarves. Her heart pounded as she hid behind the scarves, while keeping an eye on the Riders.

Did they come looking for me? Krystal wondered.

Krystal watched as Ellabeth said something to Quinn. Then Quinn pointed in Krystal's direction. Krystal held her breath. Quinn shook her head, and then they moved on to the next stall.

Krystal sighed with relief.

"You want to buy a scarf?" the merchant asked as he held up a pink scarf.

"No, thanks," replied Krystal.

"What about blue?" asked the merchant. "It matches your eyes."

Krystal backed away. "Sorry, I don't have any money," she said. As she backed away, her boot got caught in her long skirt, and she tripped over a large bouquet of flowers that was set up at the booth next door.

"Watch out!" the florist shouted.

Heads turned. Krystal felt people's eyes on her.

"I'm sorry," Krystal exclaimed. She walked away soaked, her skirt dark with water.

She fled, zigzagging through the maze of tightly-packed stalls until she was far away from the Riders. When she stopped to catch her breath she saw a smeetle, an otter-like creature. It scurried along on all fours on the end of a leash. Krystal gasped in surprise. She'd never seen a tame smeetle before.

The smeetle's collar was crusted with diamonds. Krystal wondered if they were real. When the boy holding the smeetle's leash stopped to barter at a stand, the tiny creature scampered over to Krystal.

"Aren't you the sweetest thing?" Krystal petted the smeetle's soft head.

"Don't!" the boy snapped.

Krystal's hand shot back.

"Delicia is trained only to allow me to pet her," he said.

Krystal studied the boy. He was handsome with piercing blue eyes and thick, black hair. He wore black pants and a green shirt. He also carried a cane with a silver handle shaped like a smeetle's head.

"She looks so friendly," Krystal said.

"Looks can be deceiving, fair one," the boy said. "Delicia looks delightful, but her nips can hurt."

"Oh, I've had worse. Besides Obeck —" Krystal paused. If she mentioned Obecky and her special healing powers, the boy would realize who she was. She wanted him to think she was a normal girl. She wanted to feel like her old self again.

"I mean," she corrected herself, "my mother always tells me to be careful around strange animals, but I can never resist them."

"So you're an animal lover?" the boy asked. "I have others if you'd like to see them."

"Oh, I don't —"

"What can it hurt?" the boy insisted. "We have some amazing animals from all across the eight kingdoms. Some you may not have even seen before. They are very special."

Krystal raised an eyebrow. "Really?" she asked.

"Really," he said. "I lead a group of traveling performers, you see, and we have lots of talented creatures in our acts. Plus, a few talented humans, too. You look like a performer, by the graceful way you hold yourself."

"You can tell?" Krystal asked.

"Sure I can," he said. "Are you a dancer? Or a singer?"

Krystal's chin lifted. "Both," she replied.

"Then you should definitely meet the others," he said.

Krystal thought she saw a flash of red from the boy's cane. Her training as a Unicorn Rider had taught her to question everything. But this boy seemed so genuine and kind.

Surely I don't need to be suspicious of him, she thought. I probably just imagined the red flash.

"One question first," she said. "How come you're the leader of your group? You look rather young."

The boy smiled disarmingly. "It pays to be young when you're in my line of business, fair one," he replied. "I learned many skills from my old master before he retired, and now I like being independent. So will you come?"

"All right," Krystal agreed. "Like you said, what can it hurt?"

"Fabulous!" the boy exclaimed. "Delicia, lead the way."

Krystal fell into step beside the boy. She noticed he leaned heavily on his cane. She glanced away when she caught him staring.

"I'm Dezoban," he said.

"Nice to meet you, Dezoban," said Krystal. "I'm Rhama."

• CHAPTER 5 •

DEZOBAN LED KRYSTAL FAR away from the bazaar and the crowds.

"Is it much further?" she asked.

"A little," Dezoban said. He smiled and tipped his cane at her. Krystal felt an instantly calm.

Did something strange just happen? Krystal thought. She shook her head.

You don't know this boy, Krystal thought. *He could be taking you anywhere. You should be with the others.*

As Krystal was considering turning back, Dezoban led her through a gate into a brightly tiled courtyard, known as a riad. The riad was surrounded on all sides by an orange three-story building.

43

The scent of citrus blossoms and gardenias filled the air. The courtyard and balconies were packed with spectators. Jugglers, acrobats, and dancers performed in small groups.

Among it all, a fountain bubbled away. Three marble dolphins rose from the center of the pool, standing on their tails and rotating slowly. Water spurted from the dolphins' mouths, swaying left and right and up and down in time to music that played from somewhere.

I don't know what I was worried about, Krystal thought. *This place is beautiful.*

She turned to Dezoban. "I've heard of musical fountains, but this is the first one I've seen," she said. "How does it work?"

Dezoban winked. "That is a secret," he replied.

The crowd let out a collective gasp. Krystal turned to see trainers leading animals into the courtyard.

Brightly-colored parrots performed aerial tricks. A group of spider monkeys delighted everyone with their daring trapeze act. And when two tiny gray, wrinkled creatures were led in, the crowd burst into enthusiastic applause.

"Are they elephantines?" Krystal asked.

Dezoban nodded. "Yes, they are miniature elephants," he said. "Aren't they incredible?"

The elephantines were the size of cats. They did all sorts of juggling tricks, tossing colored leather balls to each other using their long, flexible trunks.

Next, an enormous white tiger bounded into the court, his blue eyes dazzling and his tail held high. The tiger roared. People in the crowd screamed and scattered in all directions.

Instinctively, Krystal struck a defensive pose. Feet apart, knees bent, she held her hands up to protect herself. Her mind raced as she tried to think of some way to scare the animal away so it wouldn't hurt anyone.

Dezoban calmly stepped toward the huge beast. "Down, Richelieu," he commanded.

The tiger promptly sat, idly licking his paws and curling his tail from side to side. Krystal dropped her arms and pretended to straighten her skirt. She hoped Dezoban hadn't noticed her reaction. A normal girl wouldn't have tried to defend herself as she had. A normal girl would have run.

A boy sprinted over. "A thousand apologies!" he said. "I got held up, and Richelieu was more impatient to begin his act than usual."

"You must take more care, Gelsan," Dezoban said.

"Of course," he said. "I'm sorry." Bowing as he went, the boy led the tiger away.

"Don't let Richelieu bother you," Dezoban told Krystal. "He's really a pussy cat. In fact, Delicia is more vicious than he is."

Delicia gave a chirrup, as if to disagree.

Krystal laughed uncertainly. "If you say so," she said.

Just then, a girl glided into the courtyard wearing a gold coat and gold pants. The girl's hair and skin were dark like Rhama's. For a moment, Krystal thought it *was* Rhama. Then she realized the girl was smaller and younger, and her eyes were gold, not green.

Could she be Rhama's missing sister? Krystal wondered.

Krystal watched as the girl placed a silver chest on the ground and opened it. It was empty, except for its blue velvet lining. The girl stood tall, her hands pressed together in front of her as if in prayer. A silver bracelet with a peacock charm dangled from the girl's wrist.

Krystal gasped. It was the same bracelet she had seen at the markets.

The girl began to sing. The fountain danced in time to her voice. Krystal experienced a strange tugging, deep in her chest. A feeling of warmth, well-being, and the need to give overcame her. She thought maybe the girl's voice was casting a spell on her and yet, she could do nothing to resist it. She glanced around and saw that the people standing nearby seemed as enchanted with the girl's singing as she was.

Is this some kind of magic? Krystal wondered. If it is, Willow and the others should know about it. Jala, too, in case it turns out to be dangerous.

When the song ended, the people gathered around the girl and reached for their purses. Some

threw silver and gold coins into the chest at the girl's feet. Others tossed rings, bracelets, and necklaces set with rubies, diamonds, and sapphires.

Krystal scratched her head. *The girl has a beautiful voice, but is a song worth that much?*

She felt Dezoban's eyes on her. He lifted his cane. Krystal thought she saw a flash of red, but it was gone too quickly for her to be sure.

A wave of contentment washed over her. Her worries evaporated.

Never mind, she thought. The girl probably works hard and deserves those riches.

"That completes today's entertainment," Dezoban announced. "We shall see you all again soon. We'll be here for a few more days. And please, tell your family and friends."

The crowd groaned with disappointment then filed out through the archway. The performers and their animals returned to their quarters.

Dezoban reached for the silver chest.

Gelsan trotted over. "How much did we make?" he asked.

Dezoban glared. "Gelsan, what is lesson number one of our business?" he asked.

"Never count the earnings in front of visitors," Gelsan replied.

"Correct," Dezoban said. "Now put this away for safekeeping. You know where it goes."

Gelsan obediently lugged the heavy chest away.

Dezoban shot Krystal a sparkling smile. "Now, Rhama," he said. "Would you like to make water dance?"

"I don't know," Krystal replied.

"Don't be shy," Dezoban said. "The crowds are gone. It's just you and me."

Would it hurt? Krystal considered. *I'd like to know what Dezoban thinks about my singing. Maybe he'll recognize my talents.*

Krystal smiled. "Sure. I'd like that," she told him.

• CHAPTER 6 •

KRYSTAL FLOATED UP TO her room, enjoying the memory of each perfect note she had sung in the riad for Dezoban and admiring the beautiful peacock bracelet he'd given her.

You are the voice. You are the light. You are the song in the day. The words echoed in Krystal's mind.

Krystal looked around. *Where was that voice coming from?* she wondered.

"Honorable Rider," Rhama said as she appeared on the landing, startling Krystal.

Unconsciously, Krystal tugged her sleeve down to hide the bracelet.

"Oh, good. I'm happy the dress fits you," Rhama said. "It was left here by another traveler." She handed Krystal her uniform and coat. "I brought you this."

Krystal unfolded her shirt. It was washed and ironed and looked almost as good as new. "Did you sew this?" she asked.

"Yes," Rhama answered.

"You're very good," Krystal said. Her finger traced the diamond symbol. A bit of magic from the diamond pulsed through her. She had forgotten how strong unicorn magic was. It existed even in her uniform and the image of her symbol. It reminded her of Estrella and her mission.

"What did you say your sister's name is?" Krystal asked Rhama.

"Zaleel," Rhama replied.

"Does she look like you?" asked Krystal.

Rhama nodded. "Only she has the most striking golden eyes," she said.

Golden eyes, Krystal thought. *Where did I see a girl with golden eyes?* She couldn't quite remember.

The bracelet tingled around her wrist.

It doesn't matter. The voice inside her mind insisted.

Footsteps pounded the stairs below. "Krystal!" said Ellabeth.

Krystal quickly turned away. "I can't let her see me like this!" she said to Rhama. "Can you go downstairs and distract her for a minute?"

"Um, all right," Rhama replied. She looked uncertain, but she hurried downstairs anyway.

Krystal burst into her room, shoved the red dress in the closet, and put on her uniform. She tore her hair out of its braid. She went to unclasp the bracelet around her wrist, but something made her stop.

You must keep it on. But don't let the others see, the voice said.

Krystal grabbed her coat and slipped it on over her uniform. It wasn't that cold, but the long sleeves hid the bracelet. She studied herself in the mirror. Krystal

Pettigrew had vanished. In her place stood Krystal, the Unicorn Rider.

She stepped into the hallway, yawning and stretching as if she had just woken. "Did you call?" she asked.

Ellabeth pounced. "Finally, you're up," she said. "You've slept the day away. Willow's upset with you."

Krystal blushed guiltily. "Really?" she asked.

"Don't worry," Ellabeth chattered. "When I knocked on your door earlier and you didn't answer, I figured you were exhausted from the ride. I covered for you and told her you weren't feeling well."

"Thanks," said Krystal. "That was nice of you."

"I can be nice sometimes," Ellabeth said. "Besides, you looked pretty awful when we got here this morning. Feel better now?"

"Much better," Krystal said. "Did I miss much?"

"Tons, but we'll fill you in," said Ellabeth. "Come up to the rooftop."

"What's up there?" asked Krystal.

"Best view in the house," she said. Ellabeth grinned, then patted her stomach. "And hopefully dinner."

Upstairs, Krystal sank onto a padded bench. She leaned back and watched the servants light the lamps.

"Nice to see you've made an appearance," Willow said a little sternly.

"Sorry," Krystal apologized. "I wasn't feeling well, but I'm okay now."

"That's the important thing," said Quinn. She touched Krystal's hand. "Gee, you feel hot. Why don't you take your coat off?"

Krystal hugged her coat around her. "No thanks. I'm fine," she replied.

"Maybe some food will make you feel better," Quinn said.

Krystal nodded silently.

A waiter delivered a glass teapot filled with green tea and mint. Moments later, he returned with several bowls of delicious-smelling food.

"What is all this?" Ellabeth asked.

Krystal perked up enough to explain what each dish was. "Jamilla, one of our cooks at home came from Miramar," she said. "She always made the most delicious meals. Be careful. That one's hot."

"It should be," Ellabeth said. "It's fresh out of the oven."

"I don't mean hot to touch," Krystal said. "I mean spicy. Make sure you have yogurt with this and this." She pointed to two meat dishes. "And this one is especially hot. See these chillies?" She pointed to a bowl of bright red curry.

"I'll be fine," said Ellabeth as she took a mouthful of curry. "Oh! That is hot!" Her cheeks flushed red as she fanned her mouth.

Krystal passed Ellabeth a glass of milk. "Here. Try this," said Krystal.

Ellabeth gulped down the milk. "Ah! That's better," she said.

Krystal turned to Willow. "Did you uncover any clues about the missing children?"

"We did," Willow replied. "So far, eleven children have been reported missing. After speaking to several parents it seems they all had one thing in common."

"Which is?" asked Krystal.

"A special talent or skill," Quinn said. "One was a well-trained acrobat. Another child was a gymnast. Two other children were dancers. . . ."

"It looks like they're being kidnapped and taken out of Miramar," Willow said. "We've asked the local police to close all roads in and out of the city."

A horn sounded in the harbor. Krystal gazed across the rooftops and spotted a tall ship. The name *Nabozed* was painted in white letters on its bow.

Why is that name familiar? she wondered.

Suddenly, Krystal's earlier conversation with Rhama came back to her. "Rhama, the servant girl, said her sister is missing, too," she said.

"Why didn't you tell us before?" Willow asked.

"I haven't seen you, have I?" asked Krystal.

"I suppose not," Willow replied. "We should talk to Rhama right away."

The Riders quickly finished their meal and went downstairs in search of Rhama. She had already left for the day so Willow got her address from the innkeeper.

The Riders set out on their unicorns. The bracelet hidden beneath her coat sleeve made her wrist tingle.

Your talents are being wasted as a Unicorn Rider. You and Estrella could be so much more, said the voice inside her head.

The voice made Krystal feel a bit uncomfortable. She wondered where it came from.

Through the crowd, Krystal caught sight of a green shirt with gold stitching.

Dezoban.

 ● **CHAPTER 7** ●

KRYSTAL DUCKED HER HEAD to hide her face beneath her long hair.

"What's up with you?" Ellabeth asked suspiciously.

"Nothing," replied Krystal. She urged Estrella forward to ride beside Willow. "How much farther?"

"Should be right here," Willow replied. She stopped Obecky outside a dull-looking cottage.

When Rhama saw the Riders at her door, her eyes went wide with surprise. "Honorable Riders," she said. "What brings you here?"

"We want to talk to you about your sister," Krystal said. "May we come in?"

Rhama stepped aside to let the Riders into her small, sparsely furnished home.

"Do you live alone?" Willow asked.

"I live with my sister, Zaleel," said Rhama. "Well, I did until she disappeared. Our mother died two years ago," Rhama said. She stared at her hands for a moment. "Please, forgive my lack of manners. Would you like some green tea? Or lemon cake?"

Ellabeth looked hopeful, but Willow shook her head. "Thanks, but no. We've already eaten. When did you last see Zaleel?"

"Saturday," answered Rhama. "I sent her to the bazaar to buy fish for dinner. It's our weekly treat."

"Can you tell us anything that might help us find her?" Quinn asked.

Rhama shook her head. "The only thing I can think of is that she met a boy recently," she said. "He gave her a bracelet. I remember it because it was unusual, with glass beads and a silver peacock charm with jewels in its tail. She said he bought it at the bazaar."

Krystal tensed. "Do you know the boy's name?" she asked.

"D or B something," Rhama said. "To be honest, I didn't think much of it. Zaleel is very pretty. She has many friends who often give her gifts. They know we're poor, so they think they're helping us by giving us things."

Surely it can't be Dezoban, Krystal thought. *He's so nice. And there must be dozens of these bracelets around.* Her fingers sought the bracelet hidden beneath her coat sleeve.

Yes, yes, dozens, the voice in Krystal's mind chanted. It was growing stronger and more insistent all the time.

"What about you?" Ellabeth asked. "Has anyone given you a bracelet?"

Rhama laughed. "No one notices me. I wear tattered clothes and scrub floors for a living," she said. "But, Zaleel, she's different. She has spark. And she sings like an angel. Her voice will take her far, I'm sure." Rhama smiled sadly.

Krystal had the feeling that the girl in the courtyard was Rhama's sister. But she was afraid to say anything.

Yes, it's better if you say nothing, said the voice in Krystal's head.

"Don't worry. We'll find her," Quinn told Rhama as they left.

"I hope so," Rhama said.

"No one else has mentioned a peacock bracelet," Willow said as they led their unicorns into the stables. "But that doesn't mean it's not important. Zaleel's voice is her greatest talent. From what we've heard, the other missing children have great talents, too."

"So there's definitely a link," Quinn said.

"That's right," Willow replied. "We'll search the bazaar again tomorrow. I want to find out where that boy bought the bracelet. Perhaps the merchant will know something."

"I'm exhausted," she said. "I might go to bed."

Ellabeth looked surprised. "We haven't had supper yet," she replied.

"I'm not hungry," said Krystal.

"You've been sleeping a lot lately," Quinn said as she held a hand to Krystal's forehead. "Are you feeling okay?"

Krystal smiled. "Yes, Little Mother," she replied. "I'm just worn out. That's all."

She said goodnight and then trudged upstairs, putting on a good show of being tired. She tossed her coat and uniform on the bed.

Krystal held the peacock bracelet up to the light to admire it.

You are the voice. You are the light. You are the song in the day, the voice in her head chanted. The words filled her mind and coaxed her with their promise.

Krystal decided she must see Dezoban.

She slipped into the red dress, braided her hair, and then studied herself in the mirror.

Perfect. Now, come quickly. I need you, said the voice.

Krystal's heart thumped. It felt good to be needed.

She opened the window and peered out. All was clear. She climbed onto the roof. Music and the sound of laughter floated up from below. Farther away, waves crashed on Miramar Beach. The salty smell of the ocean filled the air.

Krystal tiptoed across the roof. When a loose tile slipped from under her, she landed on her knees.

She held her breath.

Slowly and silently, she crawled to the end of the roof. She gripped the edge and swung herself over before landing with a thud on the bricks below.

"Who's there?" the stable boy asked.

Krystal crouched behind the well. She prayed she hadn't been seen.

A familiar whinny sounded.

Estrella. Does she sense me nearby?

Long moments ticked by as the boy looked around. Eventually he wandered back inside.

Krystal slipped out into the street.

She heard a noise behind her and sped up, afraid she was being followed. The footsteps came quicker, closer. A hand gripped her shoulder and spun her around.

"Where are you going?" said a familiar voice.

• CHAPTER 8 •

DEZOBAN'S TEETH FLASHED IN THE DARK.

"I was looking for you," Krystal said, the pounding of her heart easing.

"Excellent. I have something to show you," he said.

Delicia chirped happily up at Krystal.

"What is it?" Krystal asked. She tossed Delicia a piece of bread she had saved from dinner, hoping Dezoban didn't see.

"Come," was all he said.

Krystal soon realized Dezoban was leading her toward the riad. "Are there more performances tonight?" she asked.

"There were, but they've finished now," he replied.

Disappointment burned in Krystal's chest.

She knew she had been too slow. She wondered if she had missed her chance to sing again and to earn riches like the girl in gold had.

"What's the name of the girl who sings for you?" she asked.

Dezoban waved his cane at her. "I call her my nightingale. Now, forget about her," he said firmly.

And Krystal did.

When they arrived at the riad, Krystal thought it looked more beautiful than it had during the day. Lights twinkled across the balconies and through the trees. The fountain gurgled happily. The water glowed with every color of the rainbow.

Krystal's disappointment evaporated. "It looks so beautiful!" she said.

"Wait until you see what else I have to show you," Dezoban said as he flung a door open. "This is the performers' dressing room."

Krystal gazed in wonder at rack after rack of entertainers' costumes. All of them were made of rich fabrics in vibrant colors. All had been expertly sewn.

"I've never seen such a collection, not even in my mother's closet," she said.

Dezoban showed Krystal another room piled high with hats, wigs, scarves, and shoes. Yet another room was filled with bottles of make-up, powders, creams, and perfumes arranged in neat rows.

"And last, but not least," Dezoban said as he ushered Krystal inside the final room.

Lit by several lanterns, the room glowed in dazzling colors of green, purple, red, and blue. Chests overflowed with jeweled tiaras, necklaces, earrings, bracelets, and rings. Crates of gold and silver coins sat in rows.

"Where did you get all this?" Krystal asked.

Dezoban waved her question away. "Here and there," he replied.

"Not all from Miramar?" she asked.

"No, the Silver City still has much to offer me," he said. "Speaking of which, how would you like to share in these riches by joining our troop?"

Krystal's heart flooded with hope. "You want me to sing?" she asked.

"No," said Dezoban. "I already have my nightingale."

"But I'm a better singer than she is," Krystal pleaded.

"Careful, fair one. Pride makes a person ugly," said Dezoban. "From what I've heard you're an okay singer. But you're not *that* good."

Krystal's hands clenched. Deep down she knew Dezoban spoke the truth, but it still hurt to hear it. "So what do you want me for?" she asked.

"For the special thing you can do," Dezoban answered. His voice was soft and coaxing.

Krystal frowned. "Which is?" she asked.

"Riding your unicorn," he replied.

Krystal's hand flew to her throat. "How did you know?" she asked.

"My people are everywhere, fair one, and it is my business to know all the treasures a city offers me. I have eyes everywhere," he said. "So, will you join us?"

Krystal gazed around at the treasure.

She imagined all the things she could wear. She imagined making people happy by performing with Estrella. How they would be loved!

Yet she knew it wasn't right.

"I can't," she said. "It would go against everything that a Unicorn Rider is."

"Are you sure?" Dezoban said as he led her to the mirror on the wall. "Look in here and see all you can be. All you want to be."

Krystal watched scenes play out in the mirror. She saw herself and Estrella performing to adoring crowds. She saw people showering her with gifts. She saw all of her loyal admirers.

This is what you want. This is what you were born to do, said the voice in her head. The voice drowned out all else except her longing for the life she saw in the mirror.

Dezoban waved his cane. Red lightning zapped. Krystal became completely caught in Dezoban's web of magic.

"Tell me what I have to do," she said.

The next morning, Krystal dressed in her uniform and coat and climbed upstairs to the rooftop terrace for breakfast. The other Riders joined her. Krystal poured each of them a cup of green tea, all the while chattering away.

Ellabeth eyed her suspiciously. "What's gotten into you?" she asked.

Krystal bit into her toast. "What do you mean?" she asked.

"You've hardly said a word in three days, and now you won't shut up," Ellabeth replied.

"Can't I be happy?" said Krystal. "I thought you would all be relieved that I'm back to normal." Krystal sniffed for effect, hoping to win their sympathy.

"Of course we're relieved," Willow said.

"But why the sudden change?" Ellabeth asked.

Krystal shrugged. "Maybe I got tired of feeling sorry for myself," she said.

"About time!" Ellabeth snorted.

"If you're feeling better, why are you still wearing your coat?" Quinn asked gently.

Krystal waved her away. "No reason," she said. "I just like wearing it. Now, I have a plan. I think we should go to the bazaar first thing to find the stall with those peacock-charm bracelets. The merhcant might remember who bought the one for Zaleel."

"We talked about this last night," Willow said.

"Did we?" Krystal asked. "I must have been so tired I forgot."

"You did go to bed early," Ellabeth said.

"The bazaar is close enough to walk to," Quinn said. "Maybe we can rest the unicorns."

The unicorns must come too, the voice inside Krystal's head insisted. *I need them. Now make sure it happens.*

• CHAPTER 9 •

"CAN'T WE TAKE THE unicorns with us?" Krystal asked.

Ellabeth groaned. "The streets around the bazaar are so narrow, it's hard enough to get one unicorn through, let alone all four of them," she said. "Besides, people crowd around and stare all the time. It's hard work."

"The unicorns have to come," Krystal insisted. "I've been out of sorts with Estrella lately. I want to make it up to her."

"Why don't you take Estrella?" Quinn said. "We can leave the others here."

Krystal nodded. "I guess that will be all right," she said.

The Riders headed for the bazaar, Krystal in front on Estrella. Without hesitation, she led them to the stall with the beaded silver bracelets.

"How did you find it so quickly?" Ellabeth asked.

Krystal shrugged. "Just lucky, I guess," she said.

"Have you sold many of these?" Willow asked the merchant as she pointed to a row of peacock bracelets.

The merchant grinned, showing his crooked teeth. "Those ones are very popular," he said. "My best customer bought ten or twelve of them."

Willow's eyebrows jumped. "Can you tell us anything about this customer?" she asked.

"He was only a young lad," the merchant replied. "He was well dressed, though, with a walking stick and a pet smeetle."

"A pet smeetle?" Ellabeth said, looking confused.

Krystal knew he was talking about Dezoban.

Yes, but you won't say anything or you'll ruin our plans, the voice inside Krystal's head said.

She glanced at the other Riders. She would miss them, but she knew her future didn't include them. She was meant for better things.

"Yes, a smeetle," said the merchant. "He was a superb bargainer, too. I gave him a good price."

"Did you get his name?" Quinn asked.

The man shook his head.

"Do you know anything else about him?" Willow asked.

"He mentioned he was renting a place on Radashi Street," he said. "Number 13, I think it was.

He wanted me to go there to see a show, but I was too busy."

"Thank you," Willow said. "You've been helpful."

"No problem," said the merchant. "How about you, Riders? Would you like to buy a bracelet?"

Willow smiled. "Maybe another time," she answered.

The Riders soon found 13 Radashi Street. Krystal led them inside. She hoped the others would like the riad as much as she had.

She watched as the others inspected the riad. Estrella wandered around, snorting at the gardenia and orange trees and stomping her foot.

"I don't think she likes it here," Quinn said.

"Neither do I," Willow agreed. "This place feels strange."

"It's so messy," Ellabeth added.

"Nonsense," said Krystal. She was disappointed by her friends' reactions. "It's beautiful." She didn't see the others exchange confused glances.

"Ula just sent me a mind-message," Quinn said. Ula's special skill was her ability to communicate telepathically with her Rider. "She says the circle of magic must be broken."

"All right, Riders," Willow said. "Keep your eyes open for the circle of magic."

Ellabeth looked confused. "Whatever that means," she said.

Willow cocked her head to the side. "Do you hear something?" she asked.

"Someone's calling for help," Quinn said.

"It's coming from below," Krystal said. "This way. Estrella, wait here."

The Riders followed Krystal inside. They soon found a staircase leading underground.

"I'll go first," Willow said. "Riders, stay alert."

Lead them to me, and you will have all your heart desires, said the voice in Krystal's head.

"Here. You might need this," Krystal said, handing Willow a candle she'd been hiding in her pocket.

Willow lit the candle, then led the way downstairs. At the bottom, a long tunnel stretched into the darkness. On either side, skeletons were piled high. Krystal and the others crowded behind her.

"What is this place?" Quinn whispered.

"Catacombs," Willow said.

Ellabeth's voice trembled. "Cata-what?" she asked.

"Catacombs," Krystal said. "They're underground burial chambers."

"Like graves?" Ellabeth asked.

"Exactly," Willow said. "They run under most of Miramar. Tourists pay money to visit them. Didn't you know?"

"No!" Ellabeth moaned. "That's creepy. Let's get out of here."

"I know it's creepy," Willow said, "but we'll be fine if we stick together."

"Shush!" Quinn said. "I hear voices."

The Riders continued, their boots scuffing in the soft dirt. Soon the rows of skeletons were replaced by metal cages, like prison cells. Willow gasped as she held her candle high. Inside one cage they saw children. Small hands reached through the bars.

"Are you Unicorn Riders?" a girl with black hair and golden eyes asked.

"Yes," Willow said. "Are you Zaleel?"

The girl's eyes widened. "How do you know my name?" she asked.

"We know Rhama," Krystal said.

The girl studied Krystal. "Do I know you?" she asked.

"No," said Krystal. She shrank back into the shadows and hoped Zaleel wouldn't recognize her.

"Well, well, what have we here?" a voice demanded behind them.

• CHAPTER 10 •

THE RIDERS TURNED TO see Dezoban.

"Who are you, and why are these children locked up?" Willow demanded.

"Krystal knows me as Dezoban," the boy replied with a grin. "These children work for me," said Dezoban. "So does Krystal now, and I'm afraid she's led you into a trap."

"What do you mean?" Ellabeth asked.

"Krystal?" Willow said. "Is it true?"

"Yes," Krystal replied with an emotionless voice.

"But you're a Unicorn Rider," Quinn said. "We ride as one, remember?"

"Not any more," Krystal answered. She peeled off her coat to reveal the peacock bracelet around her wrist. "Estrella and I are going to be performers in Dezoban's troop."

The other Riders immediately protested. Dezoban held up his hand to silence them. "I think it's time for me to reveal my true self," he said.

Dezoban waved his cane. The air shimmered, and he turned from a boy into a man. His black hair turned silver at the sides. His blue eyes grew colder.

Held fast by the spell over her, Krystal remained unmoved. The other Riders, however, were horrified.

"Gredd Aston, Lord Valerian's henchman!" they cried.

Gredd bowed low. "At your service, Honorable Riders," he said with a hateful tone. "I have been traveling across the kingdoms, using magic to alter my appearance and recruit children to collect treasure for Lord Valerian. Who, by the way, approaches us as we speak."

Again, the Riders yelled in protest. "No!"

Dimly, Krystal registered that it was Gredd's voice she had heard in her mind. It had controlled her, and yet, she could do nothing about it.

Quinn pointed to Krystal's bracelet. "Krystal, that bracelet is the circle of magic Ula was talking about," she yelled. "Take it off now!"

Krystal shook her head. "I can't," she replied.

"Then I will," Ellabeth said as she strode toward Krystal.

Gredd waved his cane. There was a flash of red lightning. Ellabeth, Willow, and Quinn found their hands and feet magically bound with ropes.

"Let us go!" Willow cried.

Gredd laughed. "I don't think so," he said.

"Krystal, take the bracelet off. Break it now," Quinn said again.

"She's too far under my spell," Gredd said. "I don't know how she ever became a Rider. She only cares about gold and jewelry. And about being the center of attention."

"Don't say that about my friend!" Ellabeth shouted. "It's not true. She cares about people. She likes to make them happy."

In the back of her mind, Krystal heard Gredd and felt ashamed. She also heard the way Ellabeth defended her. Something deeper and stronger than Gredd's spell made her hold onto Ellabeth's words. She knew they had come from a good place.

Images of the past flashed before her eyes. She saw times spent with Willow, Ellabeth, and Quinn training their unicorns in Keydell. She saw herself galloping Estrella into battle with the others by her side. She saw the Riders returning home together triumphant after a mission.

It was the Riders and Estrella who made her life what it was. They were what brought her happiness.

Not her looks or her voice or fine clothes or jewels. Krystal looked inside of herself and saw the truth. She fought against Gredd's enchantment with all her will.

Krystal knew that she had let her pride take over. She wondered how she could have been so selfish.

No! the voice shouted inside her mind. *The bracelet will give you all your heart desires. What greater reward could there be for your talents than gold and jewels? You can have none of these while you're a Unicorn Rider.*

Gredd turned toward the cages. "Come, children, you've played your part in my trap very well," he said as he unlocked the doors. He let them out and ordered them to surround the Riders.

Quinn leaned toward Krystal. "Ula sent me a mind-message," she whispered urgently. "She wants you to see it."

Though her hands were bound, Quinn managed to grab hold of Krystal's fingertips with her own.

Krystal felt the power of pure unicorn magic sweep up her arm to her mind. The message Ula sent her was a picture. It was a memory of Estrella with her magic sparkling as she enchanted the Stillmet villagers.

Fight Gredd's magic with all you have, Ula urged her. *He means to harm you and Estrella.*

With a jolt, Krystal realized how it must be for Quinn to communicate with Ula in this way all the time. It was so different to Gredd's dark, insistent voice that echoed in her mind. Ula's magic, Ula's voice, was so sweet and so gentle that it brought tears to Krystal's eyes.

Krystal thought of her beloved Estrella. She felt Gredd's hold over her weaken. She strained her mind hard, hanging on to the images of Estrella that Ula had placed in her mind.

"Oh, Quinn. I never knew." Krystal sobbed. Gredd's hold over her shattered, finally freeing her. She tore the bracelet from her wrist and tossed it away so Gredd didn't see.

"I'm taking Krystal and the others with me," Gredd said. "Valerian will put them to good use and, of course, he'll reward me well when I deliver your unicorns to him."

With the help of the children, Gredd forced the bound Riders into the cage. "You girls certainly won't need them any more," he said.

"We've closed all the roads into and out of Miramar," Willow said. "You won't escape."

"Don't be so sure," Gredd replied. "My master is going to be so happy," he gloated. "Your unicorns' magic will come in very handy to help him rule his kingdom and take over others. And to help him achieve everlasting youth."

"A unicorn's magic can't be taken against its will," Ellabeth said. "A unicorn would rather die than work for evil."

Gredd laughed bitterly. "My master doesn't need them alive," he said. "He only needs their horns."

Willow and Quinn gasped.

"If I wasn't tied up, I'd make you regret you said that!" Ellabeth growled.

Krystal knew she had to act quickly. She could not let Gredd win!

"Easy now," Gredd warned Ellabeth. He waved his magic cane at her until she calmed down. "Now, I'll leave you one last parting gift." He strode along the tunnel where a metal door was set into the wall. He opened the door, and soon the sound of rushing water could be heard. "This tunnel leads to the ocean. Unfortunately for you, it's almost high tide. This chamber will soon fill with water," Gredd said as he motioned for the children to go upstairs. "Good-bye, Riders."

"I'll come back for you," Krystal whispered to Quinn. A plan was forming in her mind. "First I have to clean up the mess I made." She ran upstairs after Gredd.

"Krystal!" Ellabeth screamed after her. "Don't go! You're one of us!"

In the courtyard, Krystal found Estrella waiting patiently for her. "I'm sorry, E," she whispered so only the unicorn could hear her. "I lost sight of who I am. I promise never to do that again."

Estrella rubbed her nose affectionately against Krystal's cheek. The bond between them that had been smothered by Gredd's magic was now restored. Krystal let it fill her heart like it always had.

Krystal knew there was nothing quite as enchanting as unicorn magic.

Krystal glanced around at the riad. For the first time, she saw the rusted gates and crumbling walls. She saw the cracked fountain, the dead gardenias and orange trees. She also saw that the children wore silver peacock bracelets.

I must remove their bracelets. Before it's too late.

Gredd grasped Krystal's arm. "You're coming with me," he said.

• CHAPTER 11 •

GREDD MARCHED HIS TROOP through narrow alleyways to the dock. He made sure Krystal was by his side at all times until he stopped beside a ship with the name *Nabozed* painted on the bow. It was the ship Krystal had seen from the hotel rooftop.

Krystal realized then that "Nabozed" is "Dezoban" spelled backward. She knew then that his plan was to take them away on the ship.

Gredd set the children to work moving boxes of treasure from the dock to the ship. In her excitement, Delicia accidentally scampered beneath her master's feet. Gredd tugged cruelly on her leash. The tiny animal was sent flying. "Be a good girl, Delicia, and stay out of the way," said Dezoban.

Delicia slunk away to hide behind a box. Krystal knelt down to pat her. "There's a good girl," she cooed. "Are you all right?"

Delicia chirped sadly, nudging Krystal's hand with her nose. "Delicia," Krystal said. "You're not mean at all. I bet that was another one of Gredd's lies."

"Once the boxes are packed, we'll collect the other unicorns," Gredd told Krystal. "Valerian will soon be here. I can feel him approaching. I can't wait to present him with Avamay's finest treasure. And I don't mean jewels."

Krystal nodded, pretending to still be under Gredd's spell.

While Gredd gave more orders to the children, Krystal snuck over to Estrella. "Now's our chance," she whispered. "While Gredd's busy with other things, we have to overpower him. Work your magic, girl."

Estrella immediately sent a shower of pearly-white magical sparks over Gredd.

"What are you doing?" he screamed at Krystal. "Tell her to stop!"

"No," Krystal said. "You can't control me anymore."

Gredd pushed Krystal to the ground. He waved his cane at Estrella. A blast of red lighting enveloped

the unicorn, forcing her to her knees. Estrella bravely fought Gredd's magic. She whinnied in pain.

"Stop it, you're hurting her!" Krystal screamed as she threw herself at Gredd.

"You little fool!" yelled Gredd. "You would fight me when I have magic?" Gredd aimed his cane at her. The force of his magic knocked her to the ground again.

Delicia jumped up and bit Gredd's hand. He yelped in pain and dropped his cane. Krystal snatched it and held it in the air.

"My magic cane!" Gredd cried. "It took years to find."

"Well, now you've lost it," Krystal said as she snapped the cane across her

knee. There was a zap of red lightning, a loud crackle, and then nothing. Krystal was left holding two broken, blackened sticks.

"No!" Gredd screamed.

"And now for the bracelets," Krystal said. She tore them from the children's wrists and threw them into the water.

"We're free!" the children cheered. "We're sorry for what we did. We had no choice."

"I know," Krystal said. "Gredd's magic fooled us all."

Estrella regained her strength and scrambled to her feet, her pearly-white magic whirling.

Gredd swayed, but still he fought Estrella's magic.

"Try to hold him, E," Krystal said desperately. "I'll run and get the others."

"It's too late!" Gredd cried. "I'll be gone before you get back. Who will come with me? Enchanted or not?"

One child stepped forward.

"Gelsan!" Krystal shouted. "Think about what you are about to do!"

"I am," Gelsan replied. "I'm nothing here. At least with Gredd I'm a tamer of tigers."

"Wise choice, lad," Gredd said. "It's time we departed this dismal shore. It's a pity we can't take the unicorns. Master will be very upset. Perhaps next time . . ." He leaped onto the ship taking Gelsan with him. "Farewell, fair one."

Creaking and groaning, and with sea water dripping from bow to stern, the ship rose into the air. Krystal gasped in shock.

More magic. If he can command a ship to do this, he has strong powers indeed, Krystal thought. *Or perhaps he was using Lord Valerian's magic.*

The ship rose higher. Krystal tried to think of a way to stop it, but it was too big and too fast. Within seconds, it had floated silently and swiftly out to sea. Krystal could only watch in awe as it disappeared.

Our Leader, Jala, must hear about this, she thought. *But first I have to save the Riders.*

She turned to Zaleel. "Wait here with the others," she said. "I'll be back soon. Right now, I have to save my friends."

Krystal leaped onto Estrella and galloped through the streets toward the riad. In one place, the crowd was so thick it was impossible to get through.

"Use your magic, E," Krystal commanded.

Estrella sent a shower of pearly-white sparks from her horn. The crowd parted and then stood dazed and enchanted at Estrella's beauty.

"Thank you," Krystal said as she passed.

At the riad, Krystal raced down into the tunnel. What she saw horrified her.

The entire chamber was already full of water.

Krystal dived into the water. She swam along the tunnel as far as she could, but there was nowhere to surface. She had to turn back.

"They're dead, and it's all my fault." She sobbed as she climbed upstairs to the courtyard. She sank onto her knees and pounded the tiles with her fists. "What have I done?" she cried.

"Would you stop beating yourself up already?" said Ellabeth.

Krystal looked up to see Ellabeth and the others. They were drenched, but very much alive.

"What? How?" she asked.

Rhama stepped forward. "Excuse me, Honorable Rider," she said. "On my way to work this morning, I overheard you talking to the jeweler at the bazaar. I came here hoping to find Zaleel."

"Lucky you did," Ellabeth grumbled. "Otherwise we'd be fish food."

"Where were you when I got here?" Krystal asked.

"We were searching the building for you and the children," Quinn said.

"Then we heard you making that dreadful noise so we came down to see you," Ellabeth said rolling her eyes dramatically. "We thought we'd better put you out of your misery."

Krystal leaped up and hugged Ellabeth. "Never change, will you?" she said. "Not for all the jewels in Avamay. I like you just the way you are."

Willow shook her head and replied, "I never thought I'd see the day."

"I am so sorry," Krystal said, the words tumbling out easily. "I'm sorry for not helping more at Stillmet. I'm sorry for sneaking out of the hotel and getting caught in Gredd's web of magic. I don't blame you if you're angry with me."

"We're just glad you're back," Quinn said.

"Really, really glad," Ellabeth chimed in.

"Where's Gredd?" Willow asked. "And Valerian?"

Krystal winced. "Gredd's gone," she said. "He left before Valerian got here. I couldn't stop him. We destroyed some of his magic, but he has more. Estrella couldn't hold him by herself."

"What about the children?" Rhama asked. "And Zaleel? Are they safe?"

"Yes," Krystal replied. "Come, I'll take you to them."

• CHAPTER 12 •

"COME AND SEE THIS!" Krystal called as she ran out of the cottage.

The Riders were back in Stillmet, putting the finishing touches to the village. Cottages had been repaired. Crops had been planted. A new hospital had been built.

Willow, Ellabeth, and Quinn followed Krystal into the cottage.

"It sure is bright," Ellabeth said as she pretended to shield her eyes.

"Lemon yellow is such a happy color, don't you think?" Quinn asked.

Willow grinned. "Perfect for Rhama and Zaleel," she answered.

"I can't wait for them to see it," Krystal said.

After all that had happened, Rhama and Zaleel had decided to leave Miramar. Jala had offered them a home and work in Stillmet, and they had accepted.

Krystal had spent the last week preparing Rhama's cottage. Once the painting was finished, she would move the furniture in. One of the villagers was even making a hutch for Delicia, because Rhama and Zaleel had asked to keep her.

"I'm sure they'll love it," Willow reassured her. "When do they arrive?"

"Tomorrow morning," replied Krystal.

Ellabeth pointed to where a patch of gray showed on the wall. "You missed a spot," she said.

Krystal groaned. "How is that possible?" she asked.

"Beats me," Ellabeth said. "You usually have an eye for detail, Miss Diamond Symbol."

Jala poked her head in the door. "How's it going?" she asked.

"Good," they all chimed.

"Great," Jala replied. "Krystal, can I have a word?"

Krystal handed the paint tin and brush to Ellabeth. "Would you mind finishing that spot for me?" she asked.

Ellabeth winked. "Sure."

Wiping her paint-splashed hands on her apron, Krystal followed Jala out into the fall sunshine. They wandered down to the river where the rapids gurgled happily.

"What did you want to talk about?" asked Krystal. She was almost too afraid to ask, but her curiosity got the better of her.

"Gredd Aston," said Jala.

Krystal tensed. "I know, I'm sorry," she said. "I let him get away. I made a huge mistake. I understand if you don't want me to be a Rider any more."

Jala studied Krystal closely. "Is that what you want?" she asked.

Krystal took a deep breath. "No. I want to be a Rider," she answered. "In Miramar, I saw Gredd slip through my fingers. I saw how powerful he and Valerian are becoming, and I know we have a lot of work to do. But I'm ready for that challenge."

Jala smiled. "Good. I'm relieved to hear it," she said. "You're a good Rider, Krystal. We would hate to lose you."

"Really? You don't want to replace me?" Krystal asked. "I was so silly. So caught up in wanting pretty things."

"I'm positive," Jala reassured her.

Krystal traced the outline of her diamond symbol on her uniform. Its meaning — clarity and perfection — came back to her. "I can't believe I didn't see Gredd for who he really was," she said.

"Evil comes in all shapes and disguises. As does bravery," said Jala.

"And foolishness," Krystal added.

"Now, that's enough," Jala said firmly. "You can't let one mistake weaken your spirit. You saw the truth in the end." Jala squeezed Krystal's shoulder. "Besides, it just goes to show how dangerous Valerian really is. I'll speak to Queen Heart about all this. She may need to call a council between the kingdoms so we can investigate the threat Valerian poses. But for now, it's lunchtime. Shall we tell the others? I'd say Ellabeth's stomach will be rumbling."

Krystal laughed. "Sure," she replied. "Wait till you see her face when I tell her it's curry for lunch!"

Glossary

bazaar (buh-ZAR)—a street market

bravery (BRAVE-ery)—having courage

canter (KAN-tuhr)—movement of a horse that is faster than a trot and slower than a gallop

dedication (ded-uh-KAY-shuhn)—giving your time, effort, or attention to some purpose

enchant (en-CHANT)—under the influence of a magic spell

florist (FLOR-ist)—someone who sells flowers and plants

groom (GROOM)—a person who cleans, brushes, and cares for horses

humble (HUHM-buhl)—not thinking you are better or more important than other people

impression (im-PRESH-uhn)—what someone thinks of someone or something

inspire (in-SPIRE)—to influence and encourage someone to do something

recruit (ri-KROOT)—to ask someone to join a company or organization

riad (RIAD)—a large house or palace built around an interior garden or courtyard containing a fountain

sparse (SPAHRS)—not crowded

upstage (up-STAYJ)—to take attention away from someone or something else

Discussion Questions

1. What things distracted Krystal from realizing who Dezoban really was?

2. Although Krystal was able to rescue the missing children, Gredd got away. Do you think she could've done something different in order to catch him and save the children?

3. What things made Krystal appreciate being a Unicorn Rider?

Writing Prompts

1. Gelsan left with Gredd because he felt he was nothing in Miramar. Do you think he was happy with his decision to leave?

2. If your name appeared in The Choosing Book, would you leave your life behind to become a Unicorn Rider?

3. What do you think Gredd and Valerian will do next in their attempts to try and take over Avamay?

UNICORN RIDERS

COLLECT THE SERIES!